If you're not from the prairie...

For my Mom and Dad, who, unlike so many others, chose to remain on the prairies.

—David Bouchard

To the memory of my parents, Christian and Philomena Ripplinger, prairie pioneers.

—Henry Ripplinger

Prairie Sky

If you're not from the prairie...

DAVID BOUCHARD
Story

HENRY RIPPLINGER
Images

Time Out

If you're not from the prairie...

RAINCOAST BOOKS

Vancouver

If you're not from the prairie,
You don't know the sun,
You *can't* know the sun.

Diamonds that bounce off crisp winter snow,
Warm waters in dugouts and lakes that we know.
The sun is our friend from when we are young,
A child of the prairie is part of the sun.

Spring Thaw

If you're not from the prairie,
You *don't* know the sun.

Skipping Stones

If you're not from the prairie,
You don't know the wind,
You can't know the wind.

Our cold winds of winter cut right to the core,
Hot summer wind devils can blow down the door.
As children we know when we play any game,
The wind will be there, yet we play just the same.

Flying the Kite

If you're not from the prairie,
You don't know the wind.

Following the Wind

If you're not from the prairie,
You don't know the sky,
You *can't* know the sky.

The bold prairie sky is clear, bright and blue,
Though sometimes cloud messages give us a clue.
Monstrous grey mushrooms can hint of a storm,
Or painted pink feathers say goodbye to the warm.

If you're not from the prairie,
You *don't* know the sky.

Harvest Time

After the Storm

If you're not from the prairie,
You don't know what's flat,
You've *never* seen flat.

When travellers pass through across our great plain,
They all view our home, they all say the same:
"It's simple and flat!" They've not learned to see,
The particular beauty that's now part of me.

If you're not from the prairie,
You *don't* know what's flat.

Abandoned Pump

Prairie Harvest

If you're not from the prairie,
You've not heard the grass,
You've never *heard* grass.

In strong summer winds, the grains and grass bend
And sway to a dance that seems never to end.
It whispers its secrets — they tell of this land
And the rhythm of life played by nature's own hand.

Day's End

If you're not from the prairie,
You've never *heard* grass.

Sharing Secrets

So you're not from the prairie,
And yet you know snow.
You *think* you know snow?

Blizzards bring danger, as legends have told,
In deep drifts we roughhouse, ignoring the cold.
At times we look out at great seas of white,
So bright is the sun that we squeeze our eyes tight.

Hockey On the Creek

If you're not from the prairie,
You *don't* know snow.

Snowball Fight

If you're not from the prairie,
You don't know our trees,
You *can't* know our trees.

The trees that we know have taken so long,
To live through our seasons, to grow tall and strong.
They're loved and they're treasured, we watched as they grew,
We knew they were special — the prairie has few.

Backyard Climbing Tree

If you're not from the prairie,
You *don't* know our trees.

Our Tree Swing

Still, you're not from the prairie,
And yet you know cold....
You say you've *been* cold?

Do you know what to do to relieve so much pain
Of burning from deep down that drives you insane?
Your ears and your hands, right into your toes —
A child who's been cold on the prairie will know!

Of all of those memories we share when we're old,
None are more clear than that hard bitter cold.
You'll not find among us a soul who can say:
"I've conquered the wind on a cold winter's day."

If you're not from the prairie,
You *don't* know the cold,
You've *never* been cold!

Heading Home

A Cold Winter's Day

If you're not from the prairie,

You don't know me.

You just can't know *ME*.

Another Load for the Elevator

Exploring the Creek

You see,

My hair's mostly wind,

My eyes filled with grit,

My skin's red or brown,

My lips chapped and split.

Time Out

Henry's Field

I've lain on the prairie and heard grasses sigh.

I've stared at the vast open bowl of the sky.

I've seen all those castles and faces in clouds,

My home is the prairie, and I cry out loud.

Flat Tire

When You're from the Prairie…

If you're not from the prairie, you can't know my soul,

You don't know our blizzards, you've not fought our cold.

You can't know my mind, nor ever my heart,

Unless deep within you, there's somehow a part....

A part of these things that I've said that I know,

The wind, sky and earth, the storms and the snow.

Best say you have — and then we'll be one,

For we will have shared that same blazing sun.

Prairie Sky

Prairie Sunset

Going to School

First published in Canada in 1993 by
Raincoast Books and SummerWild Productions

This edition published in 1994 by

Raincoast Books
8680 Cambie Street
Vancouver, B.C. v6p 6m9
(604) 323-7100

10 9 8 7 6 5

CANADIAN CATALOGING IN
PUBLICATION DATA

Bouchard, Dave, 1952–
If you're not from the prairie –

A poem
ISBN 1-895714-66-4

1. Prairie Provinces – Poetry.
2. Prairie Provinces in art.
3. Ripplinger, Henry.
I. Ripplinger, Henry. II. Title.

PS8553.O759I47 1994 C811' .54
C94-910799-9 PR9199.3.B68I3 1994

ANCILLARY PRODUCTS

*Henry Ripplinger has created a number of other
products from this book, including a package of art
cards, a keepsake portfolio of posters, and limited
edition prints of many of the images. To order these
products, contact:*

Collections Fine Art Ltd.
2175 Smith Street
Regina, Saskatchewan s4p 2p3
(306) 791-7888   FAX (306) 565-8881

PRODUCTION CREDITS

Executive Producer, Designer and Editor
Ken Budd

Layout Artist
Dean Allen

Colour separations, printing & binding
Friesen Printers

PRINTED IN CANADA ON RECYCLED PAPER